For Anna, Marius, their friends, their cousins,
and all other small and large trees.

Sophie

Reycraft Books
55 Fifth Avenue
New York, NY 10003

Reycraftbooks.com

Reycraft Books is a trade imprint and trademark of Newmark Learning, LLC.
© Éditions Le Grand Jardin, 2017
www.legrandjardin-editions.fr
Translation rights arranged through Syllabes Agency, France.

Library of Congress Control Number: 2021901940

ISBN: 978-1-4788-7374-7

Printed in Dongguan, China. 8557/0221/17683

10 9 8 7 6 5 4 3 2 1

First Edition Hardcover published by Reycraft Books 2021
Reycraft Books and Newmark Learning, LLC, support diversity and the First Amendment,
and celebrate the right to read.

The Tree Told Me

Sophie Lescaut
Thanh Portal

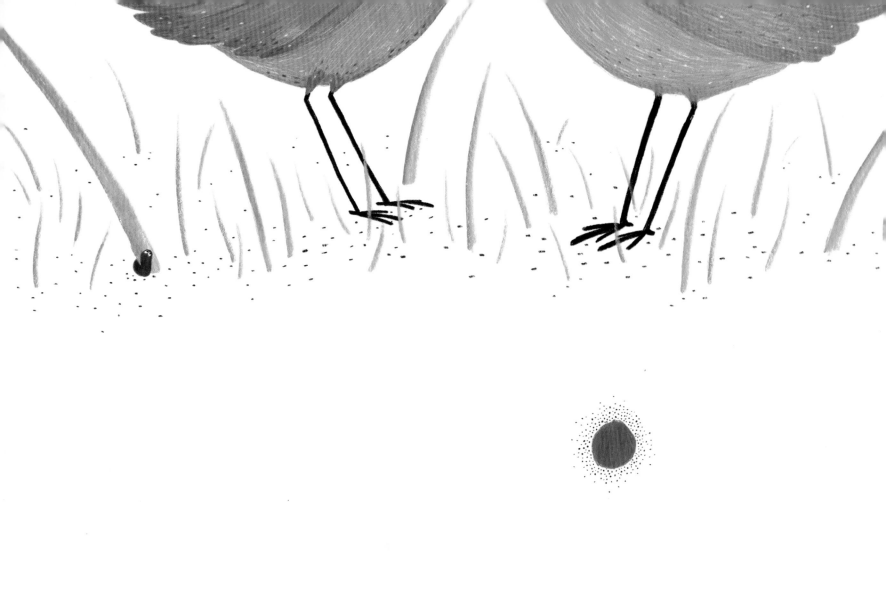

The tree told me

in the beginning we are
almost nothing

The tree told me

that we can be
strong and small
at the same time

The tree told me

to look
overhead

The tree told me

to root into
the ground

The tree told me

that there are
many ways

The tree told me

to learn to
wait

The tree told me

to share
the pleasure

The tree told me

to experience the
storms

The tree told me

that the night has its

secrets

The tree told me

that some things are
unacceptable

The tree told me

to learn how to
move
away one day